Reptile World

Tortoises

by Vanessa Black

Bullfrog Books

Ideas for Parents and Teachers

Bullfrog Books let children practice reading informational text at the earliest reading levels. Repetition, familiar words, and photo labels support early readers.

Before Reading

- Discuss the cover photo. What does it tell them?
- Look at the picture glossary together. Read and discuss the words.

Read the Book

- "Walk" through the book and look at the photos. Let the child ask questions. Point out the photo labels.
- Read the book to the child, or have him or her read independently.

After Reading

- Prompt the child to think more. Ask: Have you ever seen a tortoise? Was it wild or in a zoo?

Bullfrog Books are published by Jump!
5357 Penn Avenue South
Minneapolis, MN 55419
www.jumplibrary.com

Copyright © 2017 Jump!
International copyright reserved in all countries.
No part of this book may be reproduced in any form without written permission from the publisher.

Library of Congress Cataloging-in-Publication Data

Names: Black, Vanessa, author.
Title: Tortoises / by Vanessa Black.
Other titles: Bullfrog books. Reptile world.
Description: Minneapolis, MN: Bullfrog Books [2017]
Series: Reptile world
Audience: Ages 5–8. | Audience: K to grade 3.
Includes index.
Identifiers: LCCN 2016002938
ISBN 9781620313862 (hardcover: alk. paper)
Subjects: LCSH: Testudinidae—Juvenile literature.
Classification: LCC QL666.C584 B53 2017
DDC 597.92/4—dc23
LC record available at http://lccn.loc.gov/2016002938

Editor: Jenny Fretland VanVoorst
Series Designer: Ellen Huber
Book Designer: Lindaanne Donohoe
Photo Researcher: Lindaanne Donohoe

Photo Credits: All photos by Shutterstock except: Alamy, cover, 10, 18–19, 23br; Biosphoto, 12–13, 23tl; Dreamstime, 14–15, 23tr; iStock, 4; Nature Picture Library, 17; Thinkstock, 24.

Printed in the United States of America at Corporate Graphics in North Mankato, Minnesota.

Table of Contents

A Strong Shell 4

Parts of a Tortoise 22

Picture Glossary 23

Index 24

To Learn More 24

A Strong Shell

What is this?

A tortoise fight!

Two males stand
on their hind legs.

They bite.

They push.

Oh, no!

One lands on his back.

It is OK.

He can get up.

But he lost the fight.

The winner gets a mate.

After mating,
the female digs
a nest.

She uses her
hind feet.

She lays four
to eight eggs.

They will hatch
in a few months.

Oh, no!

Here comes a lion.

She wants food.

16

She bats at the tortoise.

She grabs with her teeth.

17

The tortoise pulls
in her legs.

She pulls in her head.

Her shell is strong.

She is too hard to eat.

She lives!

Parts of a Tortoise

carapace
The top part of a tortoise's shell. Most tortoises' shells form a high dome.

scutes
Bony, horny plates on a tortoise's shell.

beak
A tortoise has a strong, hard beak that is used for getting food and fighting.

plastron
The bottom part of tortoise's shell.

Picture Glossary

hind
Located at the back.

nest
A place or structure where eggs are laid and hatched or young are raised.

mate
A partner to make babies.

shell
A hard, stiff covering of an animal, such as a turtle or beetle.

Index

biting 7

eggs 14

female 13

fight 5, 10

hatching 14

head 19

legs 7, 19

males 7

mate 11

mating 13

nest 13

shell 20

To Learn More

Learning more is as easy as 1, 2, 3.

1) Go to www.factsurfer.com

2) Enter "tortoises" into the search box.

3) Click the "Surf" button to see a list of websites.

With factsurfer.com, finding more information is just a click away.